PRO BASKETBALL'S
ALL-TIME GREATEST COMEBACKS

BY SEAN McCOLLUM

CONSULTANT:
BRUCE BERGLUND
PROFESSOR OF HISTORY, CALVIN COLLEGE
GRAND RAPIDS, MICHIGAN

CAPSTONE PRESS
a capstone imprint

Edge Books are published by Capstone Press
1710 Roe Crest Drive, North Mankato, Minnesota 56003
www.mycapstone.com

Library of Congress Cataloging-in-Publication data is available on
the Library of Congress Website.

ISBN 978-1-5435-5433-5 (library binding)
ISBN 978-1-5435-5438-0 (eBook PDF)

Summary: Engaging text and action-packed photos describe the
greatest comeback stories in National Basketball Association history.

EDITORIAL CREDITS
Aaron Sautter, editor; Bob Lentz and Jennifer Bergstrom, designers;
Eric Gohl, media researcher; Tori Abraham, production specialist

PHOTO CREDITS
Associated Press: 9, 20, 24, L.M. Otero, 11, Paul Benoit, 14, Tim
Johnson, 17, Tony Dejak, cover; Newscom: Icon SMI/Ray Grabowski,
27, MCT/Robert Duyos, 5, Reuters/Hans Deryk, 6, Reuters/Lucy
Nicholson, 12, Reuters/Mike Segar, 22, USA Today Sports/Brad
Rempel, 28–29, USA Today Sports/Kelley L Cox, 18; Shutterstock:
dotshock, 1

Design Elements: Shutterstock

Printed and bound in the United States of America.
PA48

TABLE OF CONTENTS

INTRODUCTION
GETTING BACK IN THE GAME 4

CHAPTER 1
REFUSE TO LOSE 6

CHAPTER 2
DOWN BUT NOT OUT 14

CHAPTER 3
TURNAROUND TEAMS 20

CHAPTER 4
RETURNING HEROES 24

EXTRA POINTS
MORE GREAT COMEBACKS 28

GLOSSARY...............................30
READ MORE 31
INTERNET SITES.......................31
INDEX..................................32

GETTING BACK IN THE GAME

Every basketball fan knows the feeling. Your favorite team's shots aren't dropping. A loss seems certain, but you cheer the team on anyway, hoping that your hoops heroes can get back in the game.

Fans of the Dallas Mavericks had that sinking feeling during the 2011 NBA Finals. They were already down by one game against the Miami Heat. And late in Game 2 the Mavs trailed Miami by 15 points. But in National Basketball Association (NBA) games, teams play a full 48 minutes. The Mavs seemed finished, but they were about to stage a furious comeback.

Whether it's a single game, series, or a player facing tough odds, amazing come-from-behind triumphs are thrilling. They give NBA fans some of the most memorable moments in pro basketball.

- -

comeback—when a team rallies from behind to win a big game or make it to the playoffs; or when a player overcomes a serious injury or illness to return to the game

Led by superstar players like LeBron James, the Miami Heat were heavily favored to win the 2011 NBA Finals championship.

LeBron James

CHAPTER 1

REFUSE TO LOSE

Sometimes the odds seem stacked against you in a game, and it looks like defeat is certain. But that's when true champions are born. Players and teams often dig deep to find the spark to come back in a game and claim victory.

Dirk Nowitzki

THE MIRACLE MAVS

As the clock ticked down in Game 2 of the 2011 NBA Finals, the Dallas Mavericks found themselves behind the Miami Heat 88–73. But the Mavs weren't giving up. With 7:13 left in the fourth quarter, Dallas needed to score points—and fast. Jason Kidd, the Mavs' point guard, upped the pace of the game, and Dallas began chipping away at Miami's lead. On defense, the Mavs went on the attack to disrupt Miami's offense. It worked. The Heat's scorers went cold and started missing their shots.

With 26.7 seconds left, Dirk Nowitzki drained a three-point shot, giving the Mavs a 93–90 lead. But Miami quickly tied it. The Mavs squeezed the clock before taking the last shot. With just 3.6 seconds left Nowitzki drove hard to the hoop. He laid it in with his left hand to give Dallas the lead and the win, 95–93. In little more than seven minutes, Dallas outscored Miami 22–5. They went on to win the NBA title in six games, thanks to their magical comeback in Game 2.

EUROPEAN LEGEND

Dirk Nowitzki is just the second player in NBA history to play at least 20 seasons in a row for the same team. A native of Germany, Nowitzki became the first European player to win the NBA Most Valuable Player (MVP) award in 2007.

THE "EASTER RESURRECTION"

The 1973 Eastern Conference Finals matched the Boston Celtics up against the New York Knicks. The series saw a total of nine future Hall-of-Famers take the floor.

Game 4 was played on Easter Sunday and became an instant classic. The Knicks trailed by 16 points in the fourth quarter. As the final minutes ticked down to seconds, the Knicks staged a furious **rally** to narrow Boston's lead. Amazingly, guard Walt Frazier tied the game with a fall-away jumper with just 17 seconds left.

But there was still more drama to come. At the end of the first **overtime** (OT), Boston clung to a two-point lead with just seconds to go. Then two clutch **free throw** shots by Knicks forward Phil Jackson sent the game into OT number two. The Knicks closed out the second overtime with an 11–4 run to win the game.

The Knicks finished the job in seven games and moved on to the NBA Finals. They then defeated the Los Angeles Lakers for the title.

- -

rally—to come from behind to tie or take the lead in a game

overtime—an extra period of play if the score is tied at the end of the fourth quarter

free throw—an unguarded shot taken from the free-throw line by a player whose opponent committed a foul

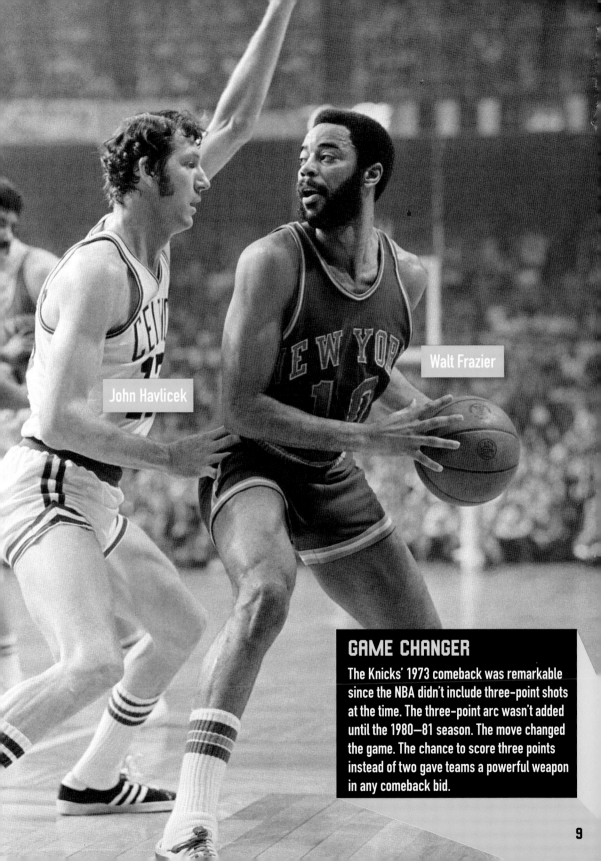

John Havlicek

Walt Frazier

GAME CHANGER

The Knicks' 1973 comeback was remarkable since the NBA didn't include three-point shots at the time. The three-point arc wasn't added until the 1980—81 season. The move changed the game. The chance to score three points instead of two gave teams a powerful weapon in any comeback bid.

ONE-MAN RALLIES

KNICKS NEMESIS

In a 1995 playoff game, the Indiana Pacers were behind the Knicks by six points with 18.7 seconds to go. Game over, right? Not with Reggie Miller on the floor. The Indiana guard hit a three-pointer, then picked off the following **inbounds pass**. He jumped behind the three-point arc, launched his shot, and sank it to tie the game. Miller then nailed a pair of free throws to win the game 107–105.

13 IN 33 SECONDS

Sometimes great players can carry their whole team. One amazing performance in 2004 turned the Houston Rockets' Tracy McGrady into a legend. With just 33 seconds left, Houston trailed the San Antonio Spurs by eight points. That's when McGrady took over the game, sinking one three-point shot after another. He even tacked on a free throw for good measure. By scoring 13 points in just 33 seconds, McGrady led the Rockets to an 81–80 victory.

----

inbounds pass—a pass to start play from a player standing out of bounds to a player on the court

Reggie Miller scored 31 points, including eight points in the last 18 seconds, to lead the Pacers to victory over the Knicks.

Reggie Miller

Greg Anthony

Pau Gasol

Kevin Garnett

Boston Celtics forward Kevin Garnett helped lead his team past the L.A. Lakers four games to two in the 2008 NBA Finals.

CELTICS ROAR BACK

No rivalry in the NBA can compare to the one between the Boston Celtics and the Los Angeles Lakers. They have faced off in the NBA Finals an incredible 12 times. The storied clubs tipped off for the title most recently in 2008.

In Game 4, the Lakers built a huge 21-point lead in the first quarter. At one point, L.A. led the game by 24 points. But then the Celtics roared back to life. They outscored the Lakers 31–15 in the third quarter to cut their lead to two.

The fourth quarter turned into a scoring battle. Boston tied the score three times, but the Lakers held them off. Finally, with 4:07 to play, Eddie House hit a jumper to give Boston the lead. The two teams fought back and forth over the final minutes. Then Ray Allen sealed the win with a driving layup with 17 seconds left. Final score: Celtics 97, Lakers 91.

The comeback from 24 points down was the biggest in Finals history. Boston went on to claim its league-record 17th NBA title.

---

layup—a close shot where a player scores using only one hand, often by bouncing the ball off the backboard and into the basket

CHAPTER 2

DOWN BUT NOT OUT

NBA teams play hard the entire season to make it to the playoffs. Once there, they play even harder. No team wants to bounce out by losing in a bad series. When teams make big-time series comebacks in the playoffs, NBA drama is often taken to another level.

Larry Bird

BATTLE OF THE BESTS

The 1981 Eastern Conference Finals set the NBA's two best teams against each other. The Philadelphia 76ers and the Boston Celtics had tied for the league's best regular-season record at 62–20. The matchup also featured two all-time NBA greats—the Sixers' Julius Erving and Larry Bird of the Celtics.

After Game 4 the Sixers had staked a 3 to 1 series lead. But Boston and Bird refused to surrender and won Game 5 on a pair of last-second free throws. Then in Game 6, the Celtics charged back from a 17-point deficit to win by two, 100–98.

With the series tied 3 to 3, the Eastern Conference championship was up for grabs. Fans were excited and Game 7 lived up to the hype. Philly led for much of the game. But in the final minutes, Bird put on a show. He led the Celtics as they reeled off nine straight points to take the lead with just 1:03 left on the clock. They held on for a nail-biting 91–90 win.

The 1981 series thrilled from start to finish. Five games were decided by just one or two points. It's often considered the most exciting playoff series in NBA history.

- -

deficit—an amount of points that a team is behind by in a game

THE "KISS OF DEATH"

During the 1994–95 season, the defending champion Houston Rockets struggled. They barely made the playoffs as a sixth seed. In the semi-final round, the Rockets were down 3 to 1 against the Phoenix Suns. With one more loss they'd be done. But they weren't ready to go home yet.

In Game 5 the Rockets roared back to win in overtime. Then they handed the Suns a loss in Game 6 to even the series and force a Game 7.

And what a Game 7 it was. Star players from both teams put on a show. But the Rockets' Mario Elie would prove to be the last-second hero. The backup guard buried a three-pointer with just 7.1 seconds left in the game. It gave Houston the lead and the win. Elie celebrated by blowing a kiss, "The Kiss of Death," to the stunned Suns' fans.

Houston's unlikely playoff run continued. They beat the San Antonio Spurs in a six-game series to reach the Finals. There, they swept the Orlando Magic to repeat as champions. It was the first time a sixth-seeded team ever won the NBA championship.

- -

seed—how a team is ranked for the playoffs, based on the team's regular season record

Houston Rockets center Hakeem Olajuwon often battled Phoenix Suns center Joe Klein during the 1995 Western Conference Semifinals series.

Hakeem Olajuwon

Joe Klein

LeBron James

"KING" JAMES

In the 2016 NBA Finals, LeBron James led all players in points, rebounds, assists, blocks, and steals. No player had ever accomplished that feat before.

LEBRON LEADS THE WAY

The Cleveland Cavaliers faced an uphill battle in the 2016 NBA Finals. By Game 5 they were behind 3 to 1 against the mighty Golden State Warriors. The team from Oakland, California had set a league record with 73 regular-season wins.

In Games 5 and 6 the Cavs' LeBron James lived up to his superstar status. He scored a combined 82 points and grabbed 24 rebounds to keep the Cavs alive and even the series at 3 to 3.

The deciding Game 7 proved to be the most exciting of all. The rival teams swapped the lead 20 times during the game. The highlight of the game came with less than two minutes to go. With the score tied 89–89, James once again came through in the clutch. During a Golden State **fast break**, James flew in from behind and spanked Andre Iguodala's layup off the glass. The play became known as "The Block," and it saved the game for the Cavs.

Cleveland held on to win 93–89. They became the first team to ever win the NBA Finals after being down 3 games to 1.

- -

fast break—an offensive strategy in which a team moves into scoring position as quickly as possible to avoid the defense

CHAPTER 3

TURNAROUND TEAMS

Watching a team come back to win a game or a series can be a thrilling experience. But for die-hard basketball fans, just seeing a team turn things around after a bad season can be fun to watch.

Lew Alcindor

LUCKY BUCKS

The Milwaukee Bucks entered the NBA in the 1968–69 season. They finished the year with a dismal 27-55 record. But then they won a coin toss to get the first pick in the 1969 NBA draft.

The Bucks chose to draft college sensation Lew Alcindor, who had won three NCAA championships at the University of California, Los Angeles (UCLA). Better known today as Kareem Abdul-Jabbar, he became the top scorer in NBA history with 38,387 points.

Alcindor was a big 7 feet 2 inches (218 centimeters) tall, but had liquid moves for a center. His signature shot was the "skyhook," and it was all but unstoppable.

The Bucks' turnaround was dramatic. In his rookie year, Alcindor led the Bucks to a 56–26 record. In the 1970–71 season, Alcindor led the league in scoring with an average of 31.7 points per game. Milwaukee finished the season 66–16. They lost only two games in the playoffs and swept the Washington Bullets to win the NBA Finals.

The Bucks incredible rise from **expansion team** to NBA champs took just two years. And it was all thanks to the talents of a game-changing big man.

SIX-TIME CHAMP

Alcindor converted to Islam in 1971 and took the Muslim name Kareem Abdul-Jabbar. Playing for the Bucks and L.A. Lakers, he won six NBA championships and was named league MVP six times.

expansion team—a new team in a league, composed mainly of players from existing teams

Kevin Garnett

Paul Pierce

Ray Allen

BOSTON BOLD

When the Celtics finished the 2006–07 season 24–48, the future looked dim. But instead of rebuilding, Boston went bold. The team traded to add star players Kevin Garnett and Ray Allen. Along with Paul Pierce, the team ripped through the 2007–08 schedule. They finished with a 66–16 record and an NBA championship. The 42-game turnaround was the biggest single-season improvement in league history.

SUPERSONIC SWING

In the 1977–78 season the Seattle SuperSonics got off to a horrible start. Sitting at a 5–17 record, they switched coaches and put Lenny Wilkens in charge. Under his leadership, they went 42–18 the rest of the way and reached the playoffs. It was one of the biggest midseason swings ever.

The Sonics ran a balanced inside-outside attack. In the playoffs, they downed the Lakers, Portland Trail Blazers, and Denver Nuggets. But their dream season finally fell to earth in the NBA Finals. The Washington Bullets bested the Sonics four games to three.

NAME CHANGERS

The Seattle SuperSonics moved to Oklahoma City in 2007 and changed their name to the Thunder. The Washington Bullets are the only team to change their name without moving to a new city. The team held a contest in 1997 to help choose a new name. More than 2,000 fans suggested names like the Dragons and Sea Dogs. The team finally settled on the Washington Wizards.

CHAPTER 4

RETURNING HEROES

Dramatic comebacks don't always involve teams turning things around. Whether they're dealing with a serious injury or facing personal struggles, athletes sometimes have to work extra hard to come back to the game they love.

Wilt Chamberlain

Willis Reed

Los Angeles Lakers center Wilt Chamberlain and New York Knicks center Willis Reed were fierce opponents during the 1970 NBA Finals.

CAPTAIN COMEBACK

The Knicks got terrible news during the 1970 NBA Finals against the Lakers. Willis Reed, the team captain and NBA's Most Valuable Player, tore a muscle in his right thigh during Game 5. Reed's hard-nosed play had helped neutralize the Lakers' superstar Wilt Chamberlain.

Without Reed, Chamberlain dominated in a Game 6 win. Wilt "The Stilt" threw down 45 points and hauled in 27 rebounds. L.A. had evened the series at three games. Without Reed, Knicks fans feared it would be more of the same in Game 7.

But during warm-ups before the deciding game, the home crowd suddenly erupted. There was Reed, in uniform, limping out onto the court! Reed scored the game's first two baskets. They would be his only points, and he only played about half the game. But his presence gave his teammates the emotional lift they needed. The Knicks knocked off the Lakers for their first-ever NBA title.

"I'M BACK"

Michael Jordan was the most exciting player of his generation. He led the Chicago Bulls to three straight NBA titles in 1991, 1992, and 1993. More championships seemed a certainty. But then Jordan suddenly announced his retirement. The basketball world was stunned. One of the greatest athletes the NBA had ever seen was walking away in his prime.

In 1994 Jordan signed on with the Chicago White Sox's minor league team. He wanted to honor his late father, who had dreamed of Michael playing pro baseball. But Jordan didn't find much success in the sport. Then on March 18, 1995, Jordan sent out a two-word statement: "I'm back." He suited up for his old team the next day. That year the Bulls surged into the playoffs before losing in the second round.

Jordan returned with a vengeance in the 1995–96 season. The Bulls cruised to a 72–10 record and blasted through the playoffs. Then they shut down the Seattle SuperSonics in the Finals to win Chicago's fourth title.

Jordan still wasn't done. The Chicago Bulls went on to win two more championships in 1997 and 1998.

----

retirement—when a person leaves his or her career and stops working

Michael Jordan

LOVE OF THE GAME

Michael Jordan retired again
in 1998. But after three missed
seasons he returned once more to
play for the Washington Wizards.
He retired for good in 2003.

EXTRA POINTS:
MORE GREAT COMEBACKS

BANG FOR THE BUCKS: On November 25, 1977, the home-court Atlanta Hawks were feeding on the Milwaukee Bucks. They led by 29 points with 8:43 left in the game. Everyone thought the game was over—until it wasn't. The Bucks outscored the Hawks 35—4 the rest of the way and pulled out a 117—115 win. It's the biggest fourth-quarter comeback in NBA history.

THE BIGGEST COMEBACK OF ALL: In a November 27, 1996 contest, the Utah Jazz trailed the Denver Nuggets by as many as 36 points. The huge lead wasn't enough for the Nuggets, though. Utah woke up in the second half. The Jazz rallied to outscore the Nuggets 71—33 and sealed a 107—103 victory. It is still the biggest comeback in league history.

COMING HOME: LeBron James grew up near Cleveland, Ohio. He was a high school star and joined the Cavaliers as a 19-year-old rookie in 2003. But as sensational as he was, James couldn't carry the Cavs to a championship. He left to play for Miami in 2009 and won a pair of titles with the Heat. Cleveland fans were heartbroken. However, "King James" came home in 2014. Two years later he led

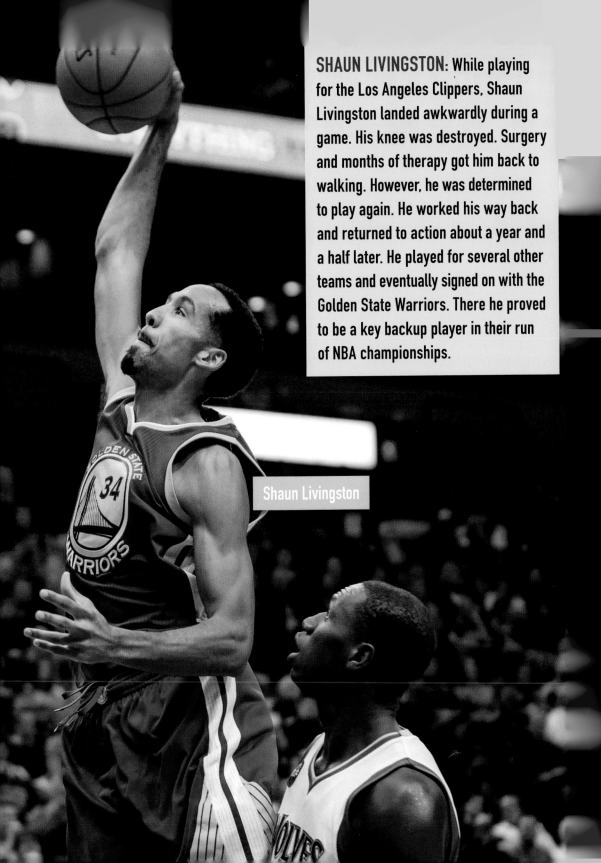

SHAUN LIVINGSTON: While playing for the Los Angeles Clippers, Shaun Livingston landed awkwardly during a game. His knee was destroyed. Surgery and months of therapy got him back to walking. However, he was determined to play again. He worked his way back and returned to action about a year and a half later. He played for several other teams and eventually signed on with the Golden State Warriors. There he proved to be a key backup player in their run of NBA championships.

Shaun Livingston

GLOSSARY

comeback (KUHM-back)—when a team rallies from behind to win a big game or make it to the playoffs; or when a player overcomes a serious injury or illness to return to the game

deficit (DEF-uh-sit)—an amount of points that a team is behind by in a game

expansion team (ex-PAN-shuhn TEEM)—a new team in a league, composed mainly of players from existing teams

fast break (FAST BRAYK)—an offensive strategy in which a team moves into scoring position as quickly as possible to avoid the defense

free throw (FREE THROH)—an unguarded shot taken from the free-throw line by a player whose opponent committed a foul

inbounds pass (IN-boundz PASS)—a pass to start play from a player standing out of bounds to a player on the court

layup (LAY-uhp)—a close shot where a player scores using only one hand, often by bouncing the ball off the backboard and into the basket

overtime (OH-vur-time)—an extra period of play if the score is tied at the end of the fourth quarter

rally (RAL-ee)—to come from behind to tie or take the lead in a game

retirement (ri-TIRE-muhnt)—when a person leaves his or her career and stops working

seed (SEED)—how a team is ranked for the playoffs, based on the team's regular season record

READ MORE

Braun, Eric. *Pro Basketball's Underdogs: Players and Teams Who Shocked the Basketball World.* Sports Shockers. North Mankato, Minn.: Capstone Press, 2018.

Frederick, Shane. *Basketball's Record Breakers.* Record Breakers. North Mankato, Minn.: Capstone Press, 2017.

Howell, Brian. *NBA's Top 10 Comebacks.* NBA's Top 10. Minneapolis: Abdo Publishing, 2018.

INTERNET SITES

Use FactHound to find Internet sites related to this book.

1. Visit *www.facthound.com*

2. Just type in 9781543554335 and go.

Super-cool stuff! Check out projects, games and lots more at
www.capstonekids.com

INDEX

Abdul-Jabbar, Kareem.
  See Alcindor, Lew
Alcindor, Lew, 21
Allen, Ray, 13, 22
Atlanta Hawks, 28

Bird, Larry, 15
Boston Celtics, 8, 13, 22

Chamberlain, Wilt, 25
Chicago Bulls, 26
Cleveland Cavaliers, 19, 28

Dallas Mavericks, 4, 7
Denver Nuggets, 23, 28

Elie, Mario, 16
Erving, Julius, 15

Frazier, Walt, 8

Garnett, Kevin, 22
Golden State Warriors, 19, 29

Houston Rockets, 10, 16

Indiana Pacers, 10

James, LeBron, 18, 19, 28
Jordan, Michael, 26, 27

Livingston, Shaun, 29
Los Angeles Clippers, 29
Los Angeles Lakers, 8, 13, 21,
  23, 25

McGrady, Tracy, 10
Miami Heat, 4, 7, 28
Miller, Reggie, 10
Milwaukee Bucks, 20–21, 28

NBA Finals, 8
  1970 Finals, 25
  1971 Finals, 21
  1978 Finals, 23
  1995 Finals, 16
  1996 Finals, 26
  2008 Finals, 13, 22
  2011 Finals, 4, 7
  2016 Finals, 18, 19
NBA Most Valuable Player
  (MVP), 7, 21, 25
NBA playoffs, 14, 16, 21, 26
  1973 Eastern Conference
    Finals, 8
  1981 Eastern Conference
    Finals, 15
New York Knicks, 8, 9, 10, 25
Nowitzki, Dirk, 7

Oklahoma City Thunder, 23
Orlando Magic, 16

Philadelphia 76ers, 15
Phoenix Suns, 16
Portland Trail Blazers, 23

Reed, Willis, 25

San Antonio Spurs, 10, 16
Seattle SuperSonics, 23, 26

the "Easter Resurrection," 8
three-point shots, 9, 10

Utah Jazz, 28

Washington Bullets, 21, 23
Washington Wizards, 23, 27